Spring for Sophie

Yael Werber

Illustrated by Jen Hill

A Paula Wiseman Book
Simon & Schuster Books for Young Readers
NEW YORK   LONDON   TORONTO   SYDNEY   NEW DELHI

SIMON & SCHUSTER BOOKS FOR YOUNG READERS

An imprint of Simon & Schuster Children's Publishing Division ❖ 1230 Avenue of the Americas, New York, New York 10020

SIMON & SCHUSTER BOOKS FOR YOUNG READERS is a trademark of Simon & Schuster, Inc.

For information about special discounts for bulk purchases, please contact
Simon & Schuster Special Sales at 1-866-506-1949 or business@simonandschuster.com.

The Simon & Schuster Speakers Bureau can bring authors to your live event. For more information or to book an event,
contact the Simon & Schuster Speakers Bureau at 1-866-248-3049 or visit our website at www.simonspeakers.com.

Book design by Chloë Foglia

The text for this book was set in Dutch Mediaeval.

The illustrations for this book were rendered in gouache with digital retouching.

Manufactured in China

1216 SCP

First Edition

2 4 6 8 10 9 7 5 3 1

Library of Congress Cataloging-in-Publication Data

Names: Werber, Yael, author. | Hill, Jen, 1975- illustrator.

Title: Spring for Sophie / Yael Werber ; Illustrated by Jen Hill.

Description: New York : Simon & Schuster Books for Young Readers, [2017] |
"A Paula Wiseman book." | Summary: Sophie listens and watches for the signs of spring—the melting ice,
the blue sky—until one day the raindrops come and spring is here.

Identifiers: LCCN 2015029656| ISBN 9781481451345 (hardcover) | ISBN 9781481451352 (eBook)

Subjects: | CYAC: Spring—Fiction. | Senses and sensation—Fiction.

Classification: LCC PZ7.1.W4366 Sp 2017 | DDC [E]—dc23

LC record available at http://lccn.loc.gov/2015029656

To my inner circle, who cheered me on the
whole way, but especially for my parents, who
have been cheering me on since day one.
—Y. W.

For Susie, a gifted puddle splasher.
—J. H.

"When will spring be here?" Sophie asked her mom.
"Spring comes slowly," her mom told her.
"How will I know when spring is coming?"

"The first way to tell if spring is coming is to listen for it. When you hear the birds start to sing their songs to each other, that's when you'll know spring is coming. That's what spring sounds like."

So, Sophie listened.

She listened in the mornings when she played with her sister in the snow,

and she listened in the evenings when she helped her dad collect wood for the fire.

At first she couldn't hear anything, except for how quiet the world was when it was covered in snow. But one day as she walked with her mom to get the mail, she heard the first chirps!

Every day she heard more and more. First the chickadees, and then the mourning doves and the robins.

Soon she could hear all kinds of birds calling to each other, announcing that spring was coming!

But outside it was still snowy and cold.

"How will I know when spring is getting even closer?" Sophie asked.

"You'll have to use your feet," her dad said. "When you start to feel the ground get softer and muddy, that's when you'll know spring is getting even closer. That's what spring feels like."

So, Sophie paid
extra attention
to her feet.

When she walked in the woods with her dad, the ground was still slippery and hard, and she had to hold her dad's hand.

When she walked Shadow with her mom, everything still felt icy. But then one day, the ground felt softer than before, and the snow was slushier, and pretty soon her boots started sinking into the ground instead of slipping on top of it.

Sophie felt
spring
getting closer.

"But it's still not spring," Sophie said, and she sighed when she had to put on her hat and gloves to go outside.
"How will I know when spring is really here?"

"Well, Sophie, you'll have to use your eyes and nose to tell if spring is here," her mom said. "You'll have to watch and wait until you see the snow start to melt. And you will have to wait until the air begins to smell like earth and rain. That's when you'll know spring is here. That's what spring looks and smells like."

So, Sophie watched.

She watched as the ice
melted off the lake,

and as the snow turned to
puddles in her yard.

She watched as flowers pushed up from under the ground and showed their stems,

and she watched as new moss covered the rocks in the woods.

She saw the world turn from white . . .

. . . to green.

And then one day, after the snow had melted, Sophie smelled the air.
She quickly put on her rain boots and raincoat, and ran outside.

Sophie looked up at the sky as the rain started to fall.
"Sophie! What are you doing?" she heard her dad call.

Sophie stuck out her tongue to catch the raindrops.

"Now I know spring is here!" she called.
"Because this is what spring tastes like!"